ON THE DEFENSE

CHICAGO GRIZZLIES

PIPER RAYNE

Cover Design: By Hang Le

1st Line Editor: Joy Editing

2nd Line Editor: My Brother's Editor

Proofreader: My Brother's Editor

ABOUT ON THE DEFENSE

Miles Cavanaugh is moving into "The Den"—a notorious four-flat apartment complex in Chicago with two of his new teammates from the Chicago Grizzlies.

The Den is known for the number of women who come and go, but as the three bachelors start their new season, they get their first inkling that things are starting to change.

Enjoy a sneak peek into Piper Rayne's upcoming Chicago Grizzlies football romance series.

ON THE
Defense

CHAPTER 1
MILES

The Uber pulls up to a typical Chicago three-flat in the heart of the north side, just across the street from the Colts baseball stadium. The driver retrieves my bag as droves of people file down the sidewalks toward the stadium, wearing red-and-blue jerseys with their favorite players' names on the back.

"About fucking time!" Siska screams from the doorway of the bar on the ground floor of the building.

I glance at the sign above my old college buddy and teammate on the Chicago Grizzlies.

Peepers Alley is the complete opposite of every other high-end bar on this street. Where everything else around here is modern, Peepers's dingy appearance makes it seem as though they're trying to be unique or stand out.

I grab my suitcase and duffel bag from the driver—all my other belongings were delivered earlier today from the rental I've been staying at since being traded to Chicago in the middle of last season.

"We couldn't have done this when there wasn't a Colts game going on?" I say from the other side of the sidewalk, then I thank my Uber driver and tip him before pocketing my phone.

"Dad! Dad!" A boy, probably about eleven, looks between Siska and me, tugging on his dad's arm. "That's Miles Cavanaugh and Damon Siska."

I smile at the kid and wink. His eyes widen and I almost laugh. I remember when I was his age and saw my first professional athlete out in the real world.

The dad is too busy hustling his family toward the stadium, talking about being late, to listen to his son, but the kid keeps looking over his shoulder.

When there's a break in foot traffic, I take the opportunity to breach the distance between Siska and me.

"Come have a beer and then I'll take you to your place." He pats me on the back as I step into the bar. It doesn't look as if it's been renovated since the building was erected.

Siska was my teammate in college, and although he can be a total dick at times, he's a good friend who always has my back. Like right now. When I first came here late last year, he welcomed me to this city like a brother. And now he's helped me get into the sought-after condo building he shares with the Grizzlies quarterback, Cooper Rice.

Each player has their own floor in the three-flat. At training camp last week, Siska informed the other players that had been bidding on the third floor that he was pulling veteran rank and getting me an in with the owner of the building after the player living there retired. Needless to say, it didn't make me the team's favorite player.

The bar isn't as crowded as the others I passed on the way here. Older men sit on stools around the actual bar, but a lot of the tables are empty. A woman behind the bar is arguing with a man at the end about the new shortstop the Colts got on a trade, Easton Bailey. She's adamant he's the player the team needs, while the guy is arguing that they need better pitching.

The guys around the bar look like the kind who've followed sports their entire lives and refer to their favorite teams with an *us* instead of *them*, as if they're on the field, diamond, or ice too. Some wear older player jerseys and I assume they must be die-hard fans.

"Rubes!" Siska shouts.

The older woman behind the bar waves at the old man she's talking to and looks at us. She has a grandma look to her, but one I wouldn't want to meet in an alley.

Siska points at me and her bored frown tips up at the corners slightly. Every barstool in the place slowly spins and all the older men are staring right at me. Whispers commence. I'm sure if they're Grizzlies fans, they probably weren't all on board with my trade even though they needed me. Their last safety was beyond his prime.

"Ah, Miles Cavanaugh, huh?" She opens the bar top to step from behind the bar and comes over to us. "It's about time you stopped in my bar."

"Sorry?" I say.

She laughs. A deep raspy one that suggests she's a smoker or was one for many years. "You don't have to be sorry, but now you're one of my boys. Any of you who live upstairs, I take care of."

Siska puts his arm around her. "Miles, this is the owner of the place. She inherited Peepers when her old man died."

Ruby gives Siska a look and he removes his arm from around her, sipping his beer. "She's not one for affection."

Interesting that she says we're her responsibility, but she doesn't like affection. I really hope the team doesn't pay her to keep track of us and every move we make.

"Nice to meet you…"

"Ruby or Rubes, I'll answer to either. Welcome to Peepers. What kind of beer do you like?"

I don't drink beer, but I have a feeling if I say that, I'll offend every patron in the bar because they all have mugs of beer in their hands and beer bellies to match.

Siska laughs, knowing I'm not big on drinking.

Ruby looks at him. "Don't tell me he's one of those girly seltzer drinkers?"

"Nah…" Though I can be and they're actually pretty good. "I'm just a water guy."

She smiles and pats my forearm. "Good for you." She waves for me to follow her over to the bar. "You don't want to end up like these guys, all looking like they've got a pillow under their shirts." She hands me a water bottle after unscrewing the cap for me. "Here you go."

"Thanks."

"Anytime." She winks then turns her attention to a grumble on the other side of the bar.

Siska leans in and says, "She's great. Nosy at times and will give you hell when you play like shit, but she's like the grandma I never had." Siska waves me toward an open doorway on the side of the bar. "Come on, Cooper is over here. You can meet his best friend."

We walk into the other room and the Grizzlies quarterback, Cooper Rice, is sitting at a table, drinking a beer and laughing with a gorgeous woman sitting next to him.

"Cavanaugh!" he says, putting out his hand.

I shake it and turn my attention to the blonde next to him. She smiles at me, and my first thought is that she's totally the kind of girl I can envision Cooper being into. She's tall with blonde hair to her shoulders and barely any makeup on. Looks like the girl next door, but I have a feeling when she's done up, she's something else.

"This is Elle." He thumbs in the girl's direction.

She puts out her hand. "Ellery actually, but call me Elle."

Then I remember that I saw her at a couple of games last year, waiting for Cooper afterward. But Cooper and I didn't hang in the same social circle after I got traded. Then again, I didn't hang with a lot of the guys. I was still getting used to a new city, new team, new dynamic.

I sit down. "What's it like to date Chicago's most sought-after professional athlete?"

Elle laughs.

"She's my best friend. It's not like that." Cooper shakes his head at me.

"I value my life, Miles. I do not like drama, and I get enough of it just being his best friend," she says.

"That's why my invitation always stands." Siska opens his arms wide.

She guffaws. "You'd be done with me after one night."

"Not you. You're different."

She rolls her eyes. "I'm sure you say that to every woman."

Siska places his hand over his heart and falls back into his chair. "That really hurts."

Siska's reputation has been cemented in the tabloids. He was a player back in college, and when I arrived in Chicago last year, I realized that nothing had changed in that regard.

We talk about the Colts season so far and how we have rooftop access to the bleachers on top of this building over-looking the stadium.

After about fifteen minutes, I'm eager to get to my place to make it start feeling like mine, so I stand. "I'm gonna get going. I want to get settled before our first practice tomorrow."

"I told you, Elle, creature of habit," Siska says.

"Oh, Miles, our friend B is coming and we're all going to the rooftop to watch the game. Want to join us?" Elle asks.

It sounds like a lot of fun, but if I'm not settled before tomorrow, my week will be chaotic and I won't function. It's imperative that I have a killer year. Being traded sucks and the last thing I need is to be traded one year after joining a new team. Then my reputation will tell other GMs I'm replaceable, and being replaceable in professional football means a shortened career. I worked my ass off to get here and I am not fucking replaceable.

"Next time, for sure. It was nice meeting you, Elle." I shake her hand and do the handshake thing with Cooper again.

"I'll walk you up." Siska waggles his eyebrows at Elle. "Make sure your friend sits right next to me."

Elle sighs. "She's already been warned about you."

Siska leads me out a back door to a staircase behind the building, and we walk up the three flights of stairs.

"How come you didn't want the top floor?" I ask.

"Fuck if I'm walking up these stairs every day."

I don't see the big deal. The exercise is good.

As if he can hear my thoughts, he says, "Yeah, perfect for your neurotic ass."

We laugh because he's right. Although I was pissed when I got traded, it's good to be here with Siska. I've missed him, and unlike my three close friends back in San Francisco, he's single like me. If I had to go to one more housewarming or engagement party, I don't know what I'd do. Being the seventh wheel isn't exactly fun, especially after your little sister finds her happily ever after with your teammate. It's kinda depressing actually.

I've decided to approach this season as a new city and new possibilities. Who knows, maybe I'll find the woman of my dreams here in Chicago. God knows it wasn't happening back in San Francisco.

CHAPTER 2
BRYCE

I stop at the corner store and grab the first Colts jersey I find in my size and take it up to the register. Baseball is okay, but it's not my preference when it comes to sports. I'm a football gal through and through. Always have been. So when my best friend from college invited me to a rooftop party to watch the Chicago Colts, I had nothing to wear. And because I am a sports lover, baseball or not, I want to look the part.

"You grabbed the last one," the salesman says to me. "Bailey is a hot commodity right now."

I nod.

I'm in the sports journalism network, so I know all about Easton Bailey coming to the Colts and how divided the fan base is, but all in all, I think his coming here is a good thing. I'd print that if I covered baseball at my new job with *Sportsverse Magazine*, but instead, I'm covering the Chicago Tundras hockey team. Hockey is second to football in my books, and I moved to Chicago and took my position with *Sportsverse* to make a name for myself, but I need to make a name for myself covering a national team. One of the big four in Chicago. But right now, all those positions are filled and I'm probably third down on the list anyway. So I'll have to continue to pay my dues with the hopes it will eventually pay off and land me a spot covering a national team.

"Do you have scissors?" I ask.

He looks at me over the rim of his glasses that rest on the tip of his nose. He's judging me as if I'm not a real fan. But nonetheless, he opens a drawer and cuts off my tag with a pair of scissors before holding the jersey out to me.

I hurriedly put it on and tie the ends to rest at my waist. He watches me with rapt attention, his judging expression evident with every raise of his eyebrow or lip.

After I pay, he holds out the receipt.

"No thanks."

One day he'll know who I am, and he won't think of me as some crazy girl fan who doesn't know stats or the players. I'm used to the judgment. Being a woman journalist covering sports, it comes with the territory.

I cross the street and follow the directions Elle gave me to the bar on the ground floor of the building Cooper lives in. I'm forced to weave through fans in red and blue since I'm going the opposite way of the stadium entrance. I repeat "excuse me" about a hundred times, only earning some grunts and sighs as I pass.

I stop outside the bar, staring at the three flats above the sign for Peepers Alley, then I look back down at the bar. I figured we were going to a modern bar like all the other ones around here, not one from the 1970s… maybe.

I walk in, earning a quirk of an eyebrow from the older lady behind the bar. As if it's a flash mob coordinated event, all the stools swivel around and a bunch of old men stare at me with their beers in hand.

"Well, we're just filled with new people today," a man says, blatantly looking me up and down.

"Turn around, darling. Which jersey you wearing?" another man asks.

Since they kind of remind me of my grandpa, I circle around, showing off the Bailey name with pride.

Half of the men grunt.

"Never mind. New to baseball, I see."

By the time I spin back around, they're all facing the televisions hanging in each corner of the bar. And when I say televisions, I don't mean flat screens.

"Actually—" I start.

"B!" Elle shouts, appearing a few feet away from me, then accosts me with a hug.

I lose my balance for a second but recover. "I just saw you last week."

She draws back. "I know, but this is like you living here now. I'm so excited to do stuff like this all the time. I'm always the only girl with Coop and his friends."

"Are you honestly asking me to feel sorry for you because you're stuck with a bunch of hot professional football players all the time?" I laugh.

She slides her arm around mine, escorting me toward the end of the bar. "Ruby, this is my best friend, Bryce. Bryce, this is Ruby."

Ruby nods. She has kind eyes even though her scowl would suggest she might not be that friendly. "I don't serve rosé, nor do I serve seltzers."

I glance at Elle, who laughs. "Don't worry, my gal is a beer drinker."

I raise my eyebrows at Elle. I'm not the keg stand, beer-bonging girl I was in college. "Um…" But it is game day and there's something about a beer with game day food that just feels right. "A lite beer, please."

Ruby grabs a glass, not frosted, and goes to the tap, filling the mug with just the right amount of head. I'm impressed when she places it in front of me. "It on Coop's tab?"

"Yep," Elle confirms, but I dig out money from my purse.

"No, let me pay."

"B, Coop makes how much per year? He'll buy you a beer." Elle shakes her head at me.

But Ruby grabs my twenty. "I like you already," she says, cashing me out at the old-school register.

She hands me back my change and I put down a tip before walking alongside Elle to wherever Cooper is sitting.

"She really is a great woman. Treats the boys like they're her own," Elle whispers on our way back to the table. "Her husband passed, and she inherited the bar years ago. Raised all her kids and refuses to do any upgrades. Says if someone can't appreciate Peepers now, she doesn't want them as patrons." Elle shakes her head, heading through a doorway to another room where Coop sits with his feet propped up on another chair, beer tipped back, watching a baseball game on an old TV.

"Look who I found," Elle says.

Coop glances over his shoulder midsip. "What's up, B?"

"Not much." I sit down to his right and Elle brushes his feet off the chair to his left.

"You look awesome." His gaze zeroes in on my tits.

"Eyes up here, asshole," I say.

"Sorry, my buddy texted and asked me about your rack. For the life of me, I couldn't remember. Now I do."

"That's because you've only ever had eyes for one of us." I glance at Elle, whose face turns bright red and she acts as if what I say isn't true.

Why Coop and Elle haven't gotten together is beyond me, but she swears they're just friends. Since they've each dated other people over the years and have both been okay with it, maybe they are. Who am I to judge?

"Who's your buddy?" I ask.

I'm crossing my fingers under the table it isn't Miles Cavanaugh. We hung in the same circles back in San Francisco and calling us enemies is putting it nicely. I almost didn't take the job with *Sportsverse* because Miles had been traded to Chicago only months before, but this is a big city and since I'm covering the Tundras, our paths shouldn't cross. As long as Coop doesn't make friends with him, that is.

"Damon Siska," Elle answers and rolls her eyes.

"Manwhore!" I exclaim and cheers Elle with the clinking of our beer mugs before we each take a sip.

"Who's the manwhore?" a deep voice asks from the arched entryway before walking in the room.

He's blond and big and his smile could just evaporate my panties, but he's Damon Siska. The man is one of the biggest players in the league.

Elle and I laugh while Coop looks at Damon. "You. Who else?"

Damon shakes his head and sits down, blatantly looking me up and down. "And you are?"

Elle and I burst out in laughter again before she says, "Damon, this is our friend Bryce."

"What happened to your friend Bea?" he asks.

I raise my eyebrows at Elle, and she shrugs like I should have expected that response. "I *am* B. As in the letter *B*, short for Bryce."

His head rocks back and he laughs to himself. "Shit, you must think I'm one of those dumb jocks."

"Never." I sip my beer and relax in my chair.

One thing about Damon is that he brings an ease and comfortableness to the room. You'd never really think I was sitting at a table with two first-round draft picks.

We talk about the upcoming season for a bit, and Damon is quick to figure out I'm not some naive girl who doesn't know anything about sports.

"Who are you really?" he asks, sounding a little suspect.

"What does that mean?"

"How do you know so much about sports?"

Before I can answer, Coop stands. "I'm going to grab another beer from Ruby. You guys want anything?"

We all shake our heads before he leaves the room, heading toward the bar.

"She's a sports journalist," Elle says to explain all my sports knowledge.

Damon's eyes widen. "Oh shit, it's you."

"Me?" My forehead wrinkles.

"You're the one who writes shit about Cavanaugh. I'm not supposed to like you. You're mean."

I roll my eyes. "I am not mean. I just tell the truth."

"All I know is the other night, he found out you were moving to Chicago, and he was not happy. We were out to dinner and I was really hoping to enjoy my steak, but all he could talk about was the fact you were moving here and how he needed to stay clear of you."

Fucking Miles Cavanaugh.

I really wish that zing of electricity didn't hit every one of my nerve endings when I think his name. It would be much easier if I actually hated him as much as I project that I do.

"Well, the feeling's mutual."

Elle glances at me from under her long eyelashes across the table. She knows Miles and I don't like each other, but she doesn't know everything. I think she's starting to suspect there might be more than I've told her.

"Then don't go up to our third floor. He's living here now," Damon says with a smirk.

My eyebrows rise at Elle. "Seriously?"

Elle points at the chair I'm sitting in. "He was just sitting in that chair."

Damn it, I knew he'd invade my group. Coop is too good of a guy. He's always taking the new guys under his wing, so it shouldn't surprise me. Good thing I'm in the hockey realm now for my job because this city is not big enough for Miles and me to coexist.

CHAPTER 3

DAMON

I'm half tempted to call Cavanaugh right now and tell him his girl wonder is down here at Peepers, but he said he might head up to the rooftop after he went grocery shopping. I think an in-person run-in between him and Bryce would be best. At least for me to laugh my ass off.

"Let's go to the rooftop," I say, pushing back from the table.

"Yeah, the game is about to start," Elle says.

"I'm watching the Reds," Coop complains because he's from some rural town in Missouri and grew up loving the Reds.

"They're losing." Elle pats his shoulder. "Come on."

He reluctantly stands because the hope of them coming back is slim. We head up the stairs to the rooftop access. Since we live here, we have six permanent seats for every game, then Ruby sells the rest of them to the public. Most of the time, it's companies buying seats for their employees.

It's awesome to meet all the different people who come to the games. I know people see me as a manwhore, but I'm an almost thirty-year-old professional football player in the prime of my life. What do they expect? When opportunity presents itself, I take advantage.

As soon as I step onto the rooftop, the heat hits me like a cloud of smoke. Holy shit, it's August and it's hot as fuck up here. I scour the area, finding some hot girls in the middle of the seating area.

A brunette recognizes us and nudges her friends, who all look over at Coop and me. She's got on a red tank top that fits her tits nice and snug. She doesn't have on a ton of makeup and her hair is pulled back in a ponytail. Her long legs are tanned and crossed, and she's sipping one of the hard seltzers from the rooftop bar that Ruby refuses to sell downstairs. What I find most appealing is that she's got that shy look that brings that flush to a woman's body that I love while I explore their every curve.

"Let's sit down," Bryce says and sits next to Elle, leaving me the seat next to her.

Having Bryce sitting next to me will make it hard to pick up someone. We look like a foursome. I have no idea how Coop does it with Elle always around. I hem and haw because I'm not sure if I'll lose the brunette's interest if I sit down next to Bryce.

"I'll catch you in a bit." I head up the stairs and sit in a vacant seat next to the brunette who was eye-fucking me. "Hey."

Her eyebrows rise. "Hey."

"Damon." I put out my hand.

She stares at it for a moment before sliding her hand in mine. It's soft and tiny, nothing like my large, calloused ones.

Her friend, a redhead, leans over. "Damon Siska, right?"

My smile grows. "Yeah. You two follow football?"

"Your reputation precedes you," the redhead says, clearly not thrilled to have me sitting next to her friend.

So I concentrate on the brunette, sitting back and crossing my legs. "So, you're a baseball fan?"

"We're here with our work."

I glance behind me at a group of guys whispering to one another and staring at us.

"What kind of work do you do?" I ask.

"Don't act like you're interested in anything other than her pussy," the redhead leans in and snipes.

"Whoa." Who the hell is this woman? Have I slept with her before?

"Isla," the brunette says to her friend.

"Seriously, you're going to sit here and go for this guy? After—"

The brunette sends her a fiery expression and the redhead shuts up, faces forward, and crosses her legs.

"What am I missing?" I ask before sipping my beer.

"I'm out of here." Isla, I guess, stands and walks down the other side of the aisle.

"What is her problem?" I ask the brunette.

"You really don't remember me?"

Oh fuck. Have I been with *this* woman before? This has never happened to me. Sure, I sleep with a lot of women, but I've never forgotten a face.

"Two months ago, we met at a bar down the street. North-sider Pub? It was after a Jaguars ball game and you took my best friend home and then asked her to leave right after. Said you had somewhere to be early and it was easier if she just went home that night. You didn't even call her an Uber." The brunette's eyes widen as if she's asking for an excuse for my behavior.

I'll admit I don't do overnights, but I usually do pay for the Uber. I bite my lower lip, racking my brain for any recollection of that night. "Are you sure it was me?"

"Damon Siska? Plays for the Chicago Grizzlies?"

I nod.

"Yep."

"Fuck, I brought her here?"

She looks at me with a puzzled expression. "No, some high-end condo with a view of Lake Michigan."

I shake my head. "Wasn't me."

"There's only one of you in this town." She sips her seltzer and shakes her head as if she's disappointed.

"Sorry, wrong guy." And it really pisses me off that someone who looks like me is out there acting like they're me.

"Can I take a picture of you and send it to her?"

"She didn't google me?" Wouldn't that be what any scorned woman would do?

"She didn't want to see a bunch of pictures of you with other women."

I shrug. "Fine."

She snaps a picture of me, and I put on my million-dollar smile. She texts it to her friend, asking if I'm the man she slept with, and we wait as the three dots appear. I try to look at the small round picture of her friend at the top of the screen to see if I recognize her, but it's too minuscule for me to get a real look.

"She says no. Damon Siska is more attractive." She laughs so hard I'm afraid she's going to spill her seltzer all over me.

"Fuck that. There is only one Damon Siska and I'm him."

"Apparently there are two and you're the less attractive one."

I grab her phone and take another selfie from my good side and send it to her friend. Her friend responds that the brunette's being duped. Pulling out my wallet, I show the brunette my license, then I google myself on my phone and show it to her.

She giggles and the sound makes me feel lighter. "Relax," she says, continuing to laugh as she goes through the Google search. "Do you ever date someone twice?"

"No." I don't play games. I tell women where it's at from the start.

"Well, seems you're honest at least."

"I didn't sleep with your friend. Does that put me back in your good graces?"

"I'm not sure. You have a reputation in this city. I don't like drama."

She crosses her legs. The movement grabs my interest, watching one leg slide over the other. They're tan and toned. My mouth waters, and for a second, all I can think of are those legs hanging off my shoulders while my face is at the apex of where they meet.

"It's called fun." I give her my panty-melter smile.

"I'll tell you what. If you can commit to sitting next to me the entire game, maybe you'll have a chance to take me to eat after it's over."

Spending hours together at a baseball game followed by dinner isn't something I normally do, but this woman has captured my interest. And who else am I going to sit with? Coop and Elle, who pretend they're friends, and their bestie Bryce who is Miles's even though he might never claim her? I've known the guy long enough to know that he's interested in her.

"Or we could skip this whole thing and go down to my place. Watch the game alone."

"Let me guess—naked and in your bed? I think you might be hopeless." She looks away from me and somehow it feels like the sun going behind a cloud.

"Let's start over." I hold out my hand. "I'm Damon."

She shakes my hand. "Adeline."

"No last name?"

She shakes her head. "No last name."

Maybe she is my kind of woman after all.

CHAPTER 4
ADELINE

Damon Siska's thigh has brushed against mine at least ten times, and each time, I lose my breath for a moment. He's so hot. How did Sami ever get him confused for some random guy pretending to be him? Even his ego and swagger are endearing to me for some inane reason.

I'm not a one-night stand kind of girl, but after my recent breakup with Peter the Prick, I think I need this tonight. A guy like Damon, who can get almost any woman he wants, is sitting next to me, flirting with me. Maybe that's pathetic, but I'm chalking it up to the huge hit my ego took when the prick broke up with me and got engaged to another woman a month later.

"So, what company do you work for? And why are all the guys scowling at me?" Damon looks over his shoulder after returning from buying me another seltzer.

"We're all teachers. One of my coworkers planned this outing for us today."

His eyes bug out. "Really?"

"What?"

"Isla is a teacher?"

I chuckle. She can be a little rough around the edges, but she's had her heart broken a lot too. "She is. We teach middle school."

"Seriously?" He balks, and I narrow my eyes. "I don't think I had any teachers that looked like you when I was in school."

I roll my eyes, but his compliment feels good. So good, in fact, that I know his chances with me are increasing. Maybe I should've told him to go to hell right off the bat. Do I really want to be another woman who doesn't make it into his phone? A forgettable face in a blur of so many others?

"Thank you, but I'm not wearing tank tops and cutoff shorts in my classroom."

"Just watch out when you wear dresses. Thirteen-year-olds are tricky motherfuckers."

He sips his beer and watches the game for a beat. I can hear his breathing, and his fingers tap on his thigh in the same rhythm they have all afternoon. He's fidgety and I wonder why. I know I can't possibly make him nervous.

"Enlighten me. Are you a sports fan?" He turns to face me.

I open my mouth and close it before responding. "I like some sports, but I don't follow the players."

He huffs. "The Bailey guy, he's good. Did you see that hard hit he just fielded and how he got to second for Reidle to throw to first for the double play?"

Maybe I should tell him the truth—I wasn't paying attention because I was wondering what it might feel like to have the weight of his strong body over mine. What it must feel like to have him thrust into me with all the muscles in his arms, back, and shoulders bulging.

Peter the Prick was the artsy type, lean-muscled like a runner, even though he never ran. And I was fine with that. I loved him and didn't care that he never worked out and hated everything outdoors. Like today, he would have never come here with me. Would have said he'd burn and that the heat gives him hives.

Damon is just different, and the more I notice things like his long fingers and the corded muscle in his forearms, the more I can't stop thinking about sleeping with the man.

"Yeah," I answer, and I think maybe I sound a little dazed.

"It was a great play, but he'll probably be ridiculed by the fans for how he played it." He leans back. "I don't know. One of my best friends got traded to the Grizzlies midseason last year and he's dealt with some shitty fans. Sometimes I wonder if it's all worth it for him."

I turn in my seat and stare at Damon's profile until he realizes I'm looking at him.

"What?" he asks.

"I don't know. This is a deep conversation to have with someone you barely know."

He chuckles lightly. "Yeah, it's just... I was downstairs at the bar before and heard all these old men, die-hard Colts fans, discussing Bailey and I'm sure in some bar last year, there were guys just like them talking about my buddy. Sometimes I want to say, get your ass on that field and let's see how you'd do."

"You should," I say, even more enamored after seeing this side of him.

Jesus, I already know I'm going to sleep with him tonight. He'd have to say something really stupid to mess it up now. But the last person I'm telling is Isla, who's gone to sit with some of our other coworkers. I will take this secret to my grave.

"They'll come up with some excuse as to why they didn't make it pro. They all always do."

"Are you sure someone out there isn't saying things about you?" I ask, clearly joking, but he takes the time to think about it.

"No, Chicago has embraced me since I was drafted here nine years ago. I hope to retire here."

We sit in silence and watch the game for a bit, but I swear I'm attuned to every minute movement he makes.

"I have to go to the bathroom," I say after a while and stand to squeeze by him.

"I'll walk you inside." He follows me.

My breathing picks up because I'm self-conscious about the way my ass looks with him behind me.

"Siska, where you been?" a guy says to our right just as I'm about to turn to head down to the rooftop bar right under the seats.

I glance over and know right away that this guy has to be another Grizzlies player. He's broad-shouldered but not as big as Damon. His dimples and killer smile are appealing but not as panty melting as Damon's. Plus, he's got a blonde tucked under his arm who is smiling at us.

"Sitting just up a few rows." Damon motions to where we have been sitting.

The guy nods.

"Adeline, this is Cooper, Elle, and Bryce. Guys, this is Adeline."

They all smile, but their expressions appear as if they're apologizing to me ahead of time.

"We're heading to the bathroom," Damon says.

"*I'm* heading to the bathroom," I say. "Nice to meet you all."

I walk down the stairway to the main bar area that has a big window looking out onto the stadium and field. I follow the signs to the bathroom and Damon says he'll get us another round.

When I'm finally alone, I go to the bathroom and afterward stand by the mirror, staring at myself, annoyed that I allowed myself to get so engrossed with Damon that I'm willing to sleep with him. Goddamn Peter the Prick. Screw him for making me feel less than and wanting a man to worship me and take away any memory of him.

"You're thinking pretty hard there." Isla stands behind me, sipping her mixed drink.

I didn't even hear the door open.

"I'm just washing my hands." I busy myself with soap and water.

"Bullshit. Everyone's talking about it." She leans her shoulder against the tiled wall. Apparently she only came in here to give me the third degree.

"About what?"

"You and Damon Siska. Henry is *very* jealous."

I inhale a sharp breath, not in the mood to talk about Henry. The man pounced on me in the teachers' lounge right after news spread that Peter the Prick and I had broken up.

"It's no one's business." I dry my hands with paper towels.

"Don't do something stupid. Taking Sami's sloppy seconds…"

I turn to face her. "Turns out that wasn't him."

"And you trust him?" Her judgmental tone annoys me. This is Isla though, and it shouldn't surprise me. But I don't involve myself in her love life.

"I do actually. He's a sweet guy."

"Come on, you're being stupid. You're smarter than to sleep with someone like him."

"Isla, this is none of your business. If I sleep with him, it only concerns me and him. I'm not looking for some white knight to save me. I'm looking for a big dick to make me scream in pleasure for a few hours."

Her mouth drops open and she stares at me. I'm not usually so vulgar, but I've had a couple drinks and she's been lecturing me on the men I choose, going on and on about how I should've known Peter the Prick was cheating on me. One can only endure so much and now I kind of want to sleep with Damon as a big fuck you to her.

I toss the paper towels in the garbage and walk over to the door.

"You're embarrassing yourself in front of everyone tonight."

"I don't really care what anyone else thinks." I open the door and leave Isla behind.

Without giving it a second thought, I cozy up to Damon at the bar. He looks at me from the corner of his eye.

"You mentioned you live in this building?" I add a suggestive tone to my voice.

He faces me quickly and stares into my eyes for a long time. "I'm two floors down."

"Then what are we waiting for?" I sip my seltzer and place it on the bar.

"Not a damn thing. Come on." He slides his big hand around mine, pulling me away from the bar toward a stairway that looks as though it's reserved for the people who live there.

A few minutes later, I'm in his condo.

A half hour later, I'm naked and screaming, just like I wanted.

An hour later, I know that I'll likely never find another lover who can please me the way he does.

Because Damon Siska does not disappoint in the bedroom.

CHAPTER 5

COOPER

think Elle is trying to slowly kill me.

She looks like a Colts fan, all decked out in red and blue, but her shorts are too short and her shirt is too tight. It's driving me crazy every time she leans over to whisper in my ear and her tit brushes against my arm.

I've attended many baseball games on these rooftop bleachers and she's never worn something so revealing. My fists have clenched so many times from watching other guys check her out. I'm one more ogle away from hauling off and hitting someone. But I can just see the tabloids. I've been there and done that before, only to almost ruin my chances of being where I am today. Lucky for me, my dream came true, but Coach Stone would not be okay with me ending up in the press for fighting.

"I'm going to get another round. You girls want something?" I ask Elle and Bryce, eager to breathe again.

"I'm assuming they aren't so restrictive up here about drinks?" Bryce asks hopefully.

"One day, I'm getting Ruby to serve a seltzer." Elle puts her hands in a position like she's mimicking swearing on a

Bible, causing her T-shirt to inch up and reveal more skin my hands itch to explore.

"Yeah, what do you want?"

"Lime seltzer would be great. I don't care what brand." Bryce shrugs.

I wait for Elle to answer, but she holds up her beer. "I'm good."

Elle's not really a drinker. The last time I saw her drunk was in college and that's a story for another time.

Walking down the stairs into the bar area, I spot Siska leaving with the brunette he was sitting with. I swear, only that guy can pick up a girl before the seventh-inning stretch.

I decide to head to the bathroom before grabbing the drinks, and a redhead plows right into me, coming out of the ladies' room.

"Excuse me," I say.

She looks up and her eyes go wide. "You people are everywhere. What the hell?" She shakes her head and walks away, back up the stairs to the rooftop.

"Okay then."

I walk into the bathroom, do my business, wash my hands, and leave. At the bar, the usual bartender, Zed, is working. He pours me my usual beer and slides it across the top.

"And a lime seltzer," I order.

He nods, grabs the drink, and rests his elbows on the bar afterward. "What's up? You look depressed."

I stare at his tatted sleeves and rebel exterior and wonder what I might have become if I wasn't a professional quarterback. What if that band I'd had in high school would've been something more than just a garage band? What if the art teacher had pushed me harder? I've been a football player since I joined peewees at the age of six.

"Nothing. Just a boring game. The Colts are actually winning and it's such a blowout there's not much action."

He nods toward the televisions above him. "Easton Bailey is, like, three for three today. He had something to prove, and he came out and proved it."

I nod. "He sure did."

"And our boy Cavanaugh will do the same this season."

"I thought he proved himself enough at the end of last season." I take a pull from my beer.

Zed shrugs. "Hard to see that when the team that traded you wins the Bowl. All people see is that they won without him."

"I never thought about it like that, but it's not because they got rid of their safety. It's because Lee Burrows is a great quarterback, and he has Brady Banks as a wide receiver."

"Don't forget Chase Andrews. They built that team to win, and they did." Zed knocks on the bar top. "And the Grizzlies' year will come soon."

"Is it every bartender's job to be this insightful with their patrons?" I ask.

He laughs all the way down to the other end of the bar to serve a woman who is standing all by herself. I didn't notice her earlier, but she wouldn't be up here if she didn't have a ticket for the bleachers. She's attractive and I'm pretty sure she knows it. She's completely done up with her hair in curls and a full face of makeup. I can't see her legs, but I'd bet she's wearing heels.

Zed hands her a drink then slides another refill my way. "From the lady," he says, winking.

I nod to her in thanks, but she approaches me and I groan inwardly, not in the mood.

"Oh, come on, smile. You're like the hot toy everyone wants to play with." Zed goes to the side of the bar while the woman who bought me a drink makes eye contact with me the entire way over.

Zed is wrong. Sure, I'm a good-looking guy and being a professional quarterback garners me some attention, but after doing a razor commercial last year, I now seem to be on every woman's radar. They do edits of me on social media, and high-level magazines are asking me for photo shoots and articles. But my life isn't what they think. Could you imagine if I told them I don't date because the one woman I want doesn't want me?

"Hi, Cooper Rice, right?" She smiles. Her teeth are white and straight, and her lipstick is a neutral shade.

I should be attracted to her. There's no reason for me not to be. I could be like Damon and take her down to my condo and fuck her. But I won't because pathetic me would rather sit next to Elle as a friend than have sex with another woman.

Goddamn, what is wrong with me?

"That's me. Thanks for the drink." I sip the beer I was already drinking.

"I'm a huge fan," she says, leaning closer to me.

She's been a huge fan ever since some woman somewhere thought I was hot and announced it to the world. I'm doubtful she follows my stats or knows I'm good in the pocket or that lately I suck when I have to run the ball. Something I need to fix if I'm gonna get us to the Bowl this year.

"Thanks."

"Welcome. Are you here with anyone?"

Bold. Sometimes I'm shocked at how bold women can be. The phone numbers slipped into our jacket pockets, sneaking into our hotel rooms during an away game, following us home. Ruby's good at chasing them away from the place the women call "The Den."

I've been excited for Cavanaugh to move in because he seems low-key, like myself. Doesn't want the girls who only want to brag they had us or post a picture on their social media while we're sleeping. Maybe he's looking for the real deal like I am—except I found the real deal and I still have to find a way to convince Elle of it.

Speaking of Elle, she walks into the bar and stops in her

tracks, noticing the woman next to me. A slow smile creeps up her lips and she gives me a thumbs-up. A fucking thumbs-up. I give her the "save me" look, but she laughs and disappears into the bathroom.

"Want to go somewhere quieter where we can talk?"

I turn my attention back to the woman. "Sorry, I'm here with some people."

"Doesn't look that way to me." She takes another step closer, and I refrain from stepping back.

"They're friends."

"We could be more than friends." She runs her finger down my chin. "Such a chiseled jaw, and those dimples, I could just lick them."

I grab her hand and gently place it on the bar. "Thank you for the drink. Let me buy you one in return." I raise my hand for Zed. "But I'm sorry, I'm not interested."

Zed comes over.

"She'll have another, Zed," I say.

Her vision locks with mine. "No, *she* won't, Zed." Her eyes turn from inviting to cold. "You know what all you athletes' problem is? You think you're so great. You get a little attention on social media, women fawning over you, and you think you're some gift to us. You probably suck in bed anyway." She circles around and stomps off, not going back to the rooftop but heading through the exit.

"Whoa," Zed says. "You really pissed her off."

Elle comes over after she gets out of the bathroom, her cute smile on display. "What happened? She was cute."

I shrug.

"Bought him a drink and everything," Zed offers up when he should keep his mouth shut.

"Coop, you gotta give these women a chance. Otherwise you're going to be alone for the rest of your life." She looks at Zed. "I tell him all the time that he should be taking advantage of these years. He's one of the hottest athletes around and I think I get more action than he does."

My fists clench and my jaw tics at the thought of someone else's hands on her.

"Maybe he's holding out for one specific woman," Zed says.

I whip my head toward him.

No way he knows. I've kept my feelings for Elle a secret for a helluva long time. But the look Zed is giving me tells me maybe he does.

"Come on, we can't leave B alone for too long." Elle walks in front of me, and I take our drinks, following her out to the rooftop and trying not to stare at her ass.

God help me. I'm pathetic.

CHAPTER 6
ELLERY

Coop and I walk back out to the rooftop, and by now, it's the seventh-inning stretch.

Bryce is talking on the phone, and as soon as we get to the seats, she stands. "I gotta go."

"What? It's not over and I thought we were going to go to dinner tonight?"

Bryce gives me the look she always does when work calls, but I can't say I don't understand. Being a doctor, I'm on call a lot. "I'm sorry. I guess some new guy just got called up to play with the Tundras and they want me to interview him for a piece tomorrow."

"They can do that?" Coop asks.

I laugh because out of the three of us, he's the one who's been involved in the most interviews for sports magazines. Doesn't he realize how important it is for the first reporter to get the story before others? But that's Coop. He's blind to his fame, which is something I've always loved about him.

"They do what they want. It's *Sportsverse*, the biggest sports magazine in the nation." Bryce hugs us both. "Love you both and we need to do this more often."

"Now that you're in our city, we can." I grin. "You're saving me. I don't have to spend all my time with Coop now." He doesn't laugh or smile, so I elbow him in the ribs. "I'm joking."

"I know," he says but still doesn't smile.

He's been off all day for some reason.

Bryce's gaze shifts between the two of us. "Okay, well, I gotta go. I'll call you both soon."

"Don't forget first game of the season."

Bryce nods, but I can tell she forgot. "Yeah, I wouldn't miss it for the world, but…" She stops herself and looks at Coop.

Miles being on Coop's team definitely makes things more difficult for Bryce. The two of them supposedly have some hatred for one another, but I swear Bryce is withholding information from me. But she didn't say anything to Coop because she didn't want Coop to automatically hate Miles when he was traded to the Grizzlies. She went on and on about how locker rooms can be tough on players when they're traded and she wanted to spare Miles any extra animosity since it's hard enough leaving his crew on the West Coast. Which, if you ask me, doesn't sound like something you'd do for an enemy, but what do I know?

I admit, hearing all of Bryce's stories of going out with the women in San Francisco, I always had a little jealousy because I wanted to be the one she was having drinks and gossiping with, so I'm thrilled she's back with me.

"Okay, I'll message you to remind you," I say.

Everyone has their roles in our friendship circle and mine is to keep us all intact.

"Great, I'll get you guys in through the back," Coop says, sitting down in his seat.

"Oh no. It's fine. We'll just meet you after the game." Bryce is quick to decline.

Coop always gets me a pass to the locker room and stuff.

Hell, Bryce is a reporter, so she probably gets them all the time too.

"What are you talking about?" Coop asks her, a perplexed expression on his face.

Sooner or later, Coop is going to figure out that Bryce and Miles have a huge dislike for each other that's going to carry on here in Chicago.

She sighs. "Nothing. Yeah, passes would be great. Since Mila Thomas covers you guys for *Sportsverse*, I can't use a work one." She smiles and waves. "See you then."

She walks down from the rooftop and I sit in my seat next to Coop. I swear he's gotten bigger every year since graduation. He's broader, more muscled, and just overall bigger. He makes me feel tiny now, even though I'm five-eight.

"So, the woman?" I turn in his direction.

He continues to watch the game since it just started again after the break. "She's not my type."

"You say that a lot, you know."

"What can I say? The women who hit on me aren't the ones I want to be with."

My forehead wrinkles. "Why?"

"Because they don't want me for me. They want me for my name, who I am in football. They want to brag to their friends. Siska might be okay with that, but not me."

"So, you want something serious with someone?"

Which is the last thing I ever want. I've witnessed enough relationships crash and burn. I don't see the point in marriage. Plus, with my schedule, no one would ever want to be with me because they'd barely see me.

"Doesn't everyone?" He sips his beer, still solely focused on the game. "Well, except you." He glances at me from the corner of his eye.

"If you'd lived through what I did, you'd feel the same way."

His hand comes to my thigh, and he squeezes. "I know.

Sorry, I'm just annoyed. Another magazine wants me to pose for a photo shoot and I'm sick of answering the same questions over and over again. I mean, it's only because they find me good-looking and has nothing to do with my skills as a quarterback."

I pinch his cheek. "They can't keep away from these dimples."

I remember the first time I saw Cooper in college. He was walking across campus, and everyone knew who he was. He was supposedly the top prospect in the nation and was going to be an amazing asset to the college's football team. We shared a class, and when he sat next to me, butterflies erupted in my stomach. Then we started studying together to pass psychology. Before I knew it, those butterflies disappeared and he wasn't just the hot jock anymore—he was Cooper Rice, my best friend. But I'm not blind. He's drop-dead gorgeous. Last year, women started doing all these video edits of him on social media, making him go viral, and now he's on everyone's radar. Which he hates of course.

"Yeah, well, dimples or not, I'm not into those women." He sips his beer.

I face forward and we watch the game, cheering for the Colts. By the ninth inning, when the score isn't even close, most people have left to beat the traffic or get an early seat at the neighboring bars.

Before the game is over, Miles Cavanaugh walks out onto the rooftop, taking in the scenery.

"Man, this is awesome," he says, coming over to us.

"Isn't it?" Coop says. "One of the great perks of living here."

Miles sits one seat away from me instead of directly next to me. Then he rests his forearms on his knees and stares at the field. He's as attractive as Cooper and Damon. It's almost like you have to be in order to be a professional football player.

One thing I've noticed from being friends with Coop and meeting a lot of professional players is that most of them struggle with their success on some level. Sure, they might be cocky to your face, but they have their own fears deep down. I'm sure Miles has some big ones after being traded and his former team winning the Bowl. There's no way that isn't crushing to an ego.

"What have you been doing since we saw you earlier?" I ask Miles.

"Just grocery shopping and getting my place together. I'm all about my routine." He shrugs and chuckles.

"That's not a bad thing."

"I guess not. But I usually get razzed about it. That, and my clean eating."

"Oh!" I shift into the chair between us. "Clean eating?"

His head rears back at first, but he nods. "Yeah, I do a lot of smoothies. Try to stay away from processed shit. Things like that."

"Me too. I mean, I'm a doctor and if you would've seen what I did in medical school, it just sticks with you." It made me neurotic for a long time until I realized that I could splurge on occasion. Come on, who can refuse sweets and fried foods for their entire life? Not me.

"Being an athlete, I just learned what my body needs for fuel to perform at my max level and it's not cheeseburgers and fries."

I nod. "We'll have to exchange smoothie recipes sometime. What's your favorite protein powder?"

We talk about frozen fruit versus fresh and all the different seeds and supplements we add in. Miles is easy to talk to and seems like a good guy all around. I'm finding it hard to understand why Bryce hates him so much.

"Game's over." Coop stands and holds out his hand. "Let's go."

"Oh." I look up. There are lots of times we've stayed out

on the rooftop after a game, finishing our drinks or just talking, but Coop looks as if he wants to leave right now. "I didn't realize."

"Yeah, because you and Cavanaugh can't stop talking about chia seeds and shit."

My eyebrows crinkle at him. What's his problem?

"Shit, I should get going anyway. Early practice tomorrow." Miles stands and puts out his hand to Coop, who stares at it for a minute before shaking it. "Thanks for having me here. I know Damon probably didn't ask you. But it's a great space."

Cooper shakes his hand, smiling at Miles, his dimples indented to the sexy level. "Yeah. No problem. Welcome to The Den."

Miles looks at me quizzically.

"That's what the women call it. You know, because you guys are Grizzlies and—"

Miles laughs. "I get it."

I nod.

"See you two later," he says.

"See you," Coop says.

After Miles leaves, Coop moves out of the way for me to go first.

"What was with the attitude?" I ask.

He sighs and walks behind me off the rooftop. "I'm just tired."

Coop acted like a jealous boyfriend, and I have no idea what that's about since I watch women flirt with him all the time when I'm standing right next to him. How does he think that makes me feel?

CHAPTER 7

MILES

FIRST GAME OF THE SEASON...

I'm a ball of fucking nerves. I don't think I've sweated this much from anxiety since my first game in the league.

When I was traded to the Grizzlies midseason last year, I was pissed off and distracted when I arrived in Chicago. I slacked, and the better the Kingsmen did during the year, the more pissed off I became. Watching your former team win the Bowl without you is soul-crushing. But I have an opportunity to make a name for myself this year and I'm not going to waste it.

"Hey, man, you look like you're about a minute away from throwing up." Siska comes over, wearing only his pants, untied.

"I've just been thinking."

"Stop thinking. That's rule number one. You're one of the best safeties in the league. *That's* why you were traded."

I'm not usually a guy who needs a pick-me-up, but it feels good to hear he thinks that. After all, the articles Bryce Burns wrote about me in San Francisco weren't exactly ego-boosting. She always harped on the negative. One positive remark and four negative ones every damn time. There were times she had a point though, and all those words and phrases have stuck with me during the years.

"Nerves?" Cooper comes and sits next to me. "I still get them before every game."

"And now you have an audience of women watching your every move," Siska says, laughing.

Cooper picks up a roll of tape and throws it at him.

"Speaking of women, you never told us about the one you took downstairs at the rooftop game?" Cooper says to Siska.

"Fuck, man, she stayed the entire night. I'm not a kiss-and-tell kind of guy, but if my condo was brand new, we'd have christened every surface."

"I ran into her when she was leaving the next morning," I say. "You could've loaned her a comb. She was trying to put her fingers through those knots."

Color had tinted her cheeks as if she was embarrassed, which seemed odd to me since one-night-stand women aren't usually like that. They're usually texting friends and snapping pictures of our places. They don't look mortified as they wait for their Uber.

"You bastard, you didn't even see her out?" Coop says.

Siska holds up his hands. "I tried, man. She was adamant that she wanted to leave by herself. As if she was ashamed of me or some shit. She wasn't ashamed when my head was between her legs."

Cooper shakes his head. "That's kissing and telling, asshole."

"It's a given that I did that when I said we had sex. Do you not always get them ready with your tongue first?"

We stare at him for a beat.

"I'm not talking about my preferences on how to get a woman off," I say.

"I second that." Cooper raises his hand, cracking his neck at the same time.

At least I'm not the only one with nerves.

"It's not kissing and telling. Maybe we can learn something from one another."

Again, we stare at Siska blankly.

"Next thing you'll want is demonstrations." Cooper stands and digs his pads from his locker before shoving them on his shoulders.

"Speaking of girls, that B friend of yours is a hot little number." Siska waggles his eyebrows and looks at me as if to confirm.

"Haven't met her yet," I say. They kept talking about their friend Bea, but she was gone by the time I got to the rooftop. "But what's up with you and Elle?"

Cooper's head whips around and his eyes hold a fiery gaze that tells me exactly what's up with them.

"Sorry, man, I was just asking," I say. "Didn't realize you were actually just friends."

"Friends, yeah?" Siska laughs, putting on his pads.

"We *are* just friends, but I'd rather not have her date any of my teammates. If things go south, it could be complicated, you know?" Cooper says.

I nod. "Sure. Of course."

"Also, because he wants her but refuses to cross the line."

"Fuck you, Siska. You have no idea what you're talking about." Cooper doesn't even bother looking at him.

"Everyone sees it. It's obvious when you look at her." Siska pretends to stare at us with puppy-dog eyes.

I shake my head. "I didn't want any teammate to touch my sister, but fucking Chase Andrews swooped in and now they're having a baby together." A full-body shiver racks my body.

"Yeah, he's got balls," Siska says.

"Well, he's Chase fucking Andrews." Cooper turns to me. "But I'd fix you up with B. She loves sports, football is her favorite, and she's just a lot of fun to be around. Not much gets her in a bad mood."

I shrug. "I guess we'll see the next time you guys all hang out."

I'm still hung up on the fact that Bryce Burns is living in Chicago now. After my sister told me that my archnemesis had moved here to write for *Sportsverse Magazine*, I was proud of Bryce because I know she wants to make a name for herself, but at the same time, I'd thought I had escaped her. That I'd be able to start over without worrying about running into her. Maybe this Bea will help take Bryce off my mind.

"She and Elle are stopping in before the game. They used to do it in college, and I thought maybe it'd give us all good luck this season if they wished me good luck before the game." Cooper shrugs. "I'm willing to do about anything to win the Bowl this year."

Siska and I nod. We both want it too, like a burning need inside us. I want it to prove my worth, Siska because it pisses him off that Lee, our other college buddy, won it last year, and Cooper because I think he wants to prove he's more than just easy on the eyes.

We continue to get ready, and once we're all dressed, we sit around in the circle. Siska and Cooper are captains, so they lead the team with a talk that should get us hyped up to win. And they each do a great job.

I grab my helmet from the locker room as the door bursts open. Standing there in team gear is Elle with Cooper's number on her cheek and a shorter woman who has the Grizzlies mascot head on as she dances into the locker room.

This must be Bea. Even with a mascot head, it's easy to see that she has a sexy body. She's wearing Cooper's jersey and her shorts show off her olive-toned legs with a pair of orange Converse. I'm already interested.

The team watches with laughter as they attack Cooper, giving him hugs.

"What the hell?" He lifts the mascot head, revealing a mass of dark hair.

When she laughs, my mouth hangs open and I realize that Bea isn't Bea. It's *B*, the first initial of the name Bryce. Her dark eyes land on me and there's no surprise in them like there must be in mine.

She knew. Of course she did. My trade to this team wasn't a secret.

"Only you, B," Cooper says and brings her over to me. "B, this is Miles. Miles, this is B." Cooper's hand moves back and forth between us.

This is a telling moment. Will she reveal she knows me, or do we act like strangers?

"Hello, Miles," she says, lips pressed into a thin line and not hiding her displeasure.

Guess I have my answer.

I give her a curt nod. "Bryce."

———

Join Miles and Bryce as they navigate love and life in a new city in SOMETHING LIKE HATE, the first full-length novel in our Chicago Grizzlies series!

ABOUT PIPER & RAYNE

Piper Rayne is a USA Today Bestselling Author duo who write "heartwarming humor with a side of sizzle" about families, whether that be blood or found. They both have e-readers full of one-clickable books, they're married to husbands who drive them to drink, and they're both chauffeurs to their kids. Most of all, they love hot heroes and quirky heroines who make them laugh, and they hope you do, too!

ALSO BY PIPER RAYNE

My Almost Ex

My Vegas Groom

A Greene Family Summer Bash

My Sister's Flirty Friend

My Unexpected Surprise

My Famous Frenemy

A Greene Family Vacation

My Scorned Best Friend

My Fake Fiancé

My Brother's Forbidden Friend

A Greene Family Christmas

The Modern Love World

Charmed by the Bartender

Hooked by the Boxer

Mad about the Banker

The Single Dads Club

Real Deal

Dirty Talker

Sexy Beast

Hollywood Hearts

Mister Mom

Animal Attraction

Domestic Bliss

Bedroom Games

Cold as Ice

On Thin Ice

Break the Ice

Box Set

Charity Case
Manic Monday
Afternoon Delight
Happy Hour

Blue Collar Brothers
Flirting with Fire
Crushing on the Cop
Engaged to the EMT

White Collar Brothers
Sexy Filthy Boss
Dirty Flirty Enemy
Wild Steamy Hook-up

The Rooftop Crew
My Bestie's Ex
A Royal Mistake
The Rival Roomies
Our Star-Crossed Kiss
The Do-Over
A Co-Workers Crush

Hockey Hotties
My Lucky #13
The Trouble with #9
Faking it with #41
Sneaking around with #34
Second Shot with #76
Offside with #55

Kingsmen Football Stars

You Had Your Chance, Lee Burrows

You Can't Kiss the Nanny, Brady Banks

Over My Brother's Dead Body, Chase Andrews

Plain Daisy Ranch

The One I Left Behind

Standalones

Single and Ready to Jingle

Claus and Effect

Made in United States
Troutdale, OR
01/11/2025

27826150R10033